HERE COME
RACCOONS!

HERE COME RACCOONS!
by LILLIAN HOBAN

Holt, Rinehart and Winston / New York

This one is for Miriam Chaikin

Library of Congress Cataloging in Publication Data
Hoban, Lillian.   Here come raccoons!

SUMMARY: Identical twins, Albert and Arabella, save their fellow raccoons from the wrath of the skunks and possums when a critical situation develops over opening garbage cans.

[1. Raccoons—Fiction.   2. Twins—Fiction]   I. Title.   PZ7.H635He   [E]
hc ISBN 0-03-017781-2   76-25205 10 9 8 7 6 5 4 3
pbk. ISBN 0-03-048951-2   79-10476 10 9 8 7 6 5 4 3 2 1

HERE COME RACCOONS!

chapter 1

Albert and Arabella Raccoon were twins. They looked exactly alike. No one could tell which one was Albert and which one was Arabella. They had the same number of rings on their tails, the same bright look in their beady black eyes, and when they lifted their noses out of their milk mugs, they each had exactly the same milk mustaches.

"It certainly is a trial," sighed Mrs. Raccoon as she mended twin jackets in exactly the same places, "not to be able to tell my own children apart."

Outside, Albert and Arabella were practicing opening garbage cans in the backyard. First Albert got on the lid and rocked back and forth. When he got the can rocking hard, Arabella stood on her tiptoes and gave it a shove. The can fell over with a crash, the lid rolled off, and Albert hopped in.

Mr. Raccoon, who was dozing behind his paper, opened one eye. He let the paper

drop on his face as the crash echoed
through the house. The night before he
had taken advantage of the full moon to go
to Possum Junction in search of better garbage cans, and he was very tired. "Tell
those twins to stop the noise," he groaned
sleepily.

"Beautiful technique," said Grandfather Raccoon, coming up the path.
"That was pretty fancy footwork, Albert."

He patted Arabella on the back. "You're a credit to your father."

"I'm not Albert, sir, I'm Arabella," said Arabella.

"Hm'm, yes," said Grandfather. He peered at Arabella over his glasses and pinched her cheek. "As I was saying, a credit to your mother."

Mrs. Raccoon came out on the porch. "Children," she called, "stop that racket. Father's trying to take a nap."

"We were only doing our homework, Ma," said Albert. "Teacher said to do three simple can-opening exercises."

"When I was young, Arabella," said Mother, "we girls were taught to do our can opening daintily, without any noise."

"I'm not Arabella, Ma, I'm Albert," said Albert.

"It's just as I was saying to their father," said Mrs. Raccoon to Grandfather. "What's a poor woman to do when she can't tell her own children apart? It does seem hard sometimes," she sighed, "not to be able to tell which is which."

"You mean who is who," said Grandfather kindly. "But don't fret, they'll change with time. Nature's bound to take her course." He settled himself comfortably into a rocking chair and looked

fondly at the twins as they helped Mother
serve tea.

"Milk or lemon, sir?" asked Albert
politely.

"And will you have one of these cream
cakes?" asked Arabella.

"Milk, thank you, and I'll have one of
the sticky buns," said Grandfather. He
took a sip of tea and a bite of sticky bun.

"Excellent sticky bun," he murmured. "Best I've had in a long time."

"Father got them over at Possum Junction," said Mother. "They have the best cakes and sticky buns there."

"Well," said Grandfather, "in that case I'll have another. It might be a long time before I get a chance to eat a Possum Junction sticky bun again."

"How's that?" asked Mother.

"What!" said Grandfather. "Haven't you heard the news? The skunks and the possums at Possum Junction have gotten up a petition against us raccoons. They've put up a sign on Main Street saying NO RACCOONS WANTED HERE."

"Why's that?" asked Father who had come out on the porch. "We raccoons have always been good neighbors to the possums and the skunks. When hard times came we always shared with them and they shared with us."

"Well," said Grandfather, "some of the skunks and possums say that the raccoons make such a mess of the garbage that people buy extra fancy garbage cans that are foolproof. No one can get the lids off, and everyone has a hard time."

"Pooh," said Albert. "No can is too hard for a smart raccoon to open."

"I bet we could open any old foolproof can," said Arabella. "We're in the advanced group of our Creative Can-opening Class."

"Quiet twins," said Father thoughtfully. "I'm afraid the skunks and possums are right. I was at Possum Junction last night. And there were quite a few cans that had those newfangled foolproof lids."

"Seems to me the best thing to do would be to fool the foolproof lids," said Mother, her eyes snapping, "instead of turning on your friends and neighbors."

"You're right, Mother," said Father. "But how are you going to get the skunks and possums to see it your way?"

"We could go to Possum Junction

tonight when the moon is down," said Mother. We could figure out how to open those newfangled lids!"

"Oh let us help!" cried the twins excitedly.

"Now twins," said Father sternly, "this is grown-up business. Possum Junction is no place for you twins to be fooling around."

"We wouldn't fool around," cried Arabella. "Please let us help!"

"Well . . .," said Father cautiously.

"Look, we have a new technique," said Albert eagerly demonstrating. "Arabella holds the can like this." He held on to the tea table. "I put one foot up." The table tilted dangerously. "Then Arabella jumps....."

"Look out!" cried Grandfather.

The table went over with a crash. Arabella, who was poised to jump, slipped on a cream cake. She skidded into Albert as he crawled out from under the table wearing a plate of sticky buns rakishly over one eye. Albert backed up and bumped into Mother. Arabella was blissfully eating the remains of the cream cake that had stuck to her foot and looked up in smeary surprise as Mother came tumbling down on her. She rolled over on her back, and her legs shot up dislodging the cream cake.

Father, who had been standing braced against the porch rail trying to keep an aloof distance, let out a muffled roar as the cream cake made a direct hit full on his face.

"AAALBERT!" he yelled through the cream, groping in the direction of Arabella.

"I'm not Albert, sir, I'm Arabella," said Arabella, fearfully peering out from behind Mother's skirts.

"I'm Albert, sir," said Albert. He pulled at the sticky buns, and as they suddenly came loose he fell over backwards onto Mother and Arabella.

"I don't care which of you is which!" roared Father wiping gobs of cream from his face. "That settles it! NO TWINS ALLOWED AT POSSUM JUNC-TION!"

"You mean who is who," said Grandfather. He stared hard at the twins over his glasses. "Someday," he said, "and I hope it's soon, Nature's *bound* to take her course!"

chapter 2

That night, after the twins had been put safely to bed, Mr. and Mrs. Raccoon and Grandfather made plans to go to Possum Junction when the moon went down.

"We'll have to be very careful," warned Grandfather. "I hear some of the skunks are setting up roadblocks."

Father was busy drawing a map of Possum Junction. "If they are guarding the roads, we'll come in by way of Duckweed Marsh," he said. "We'll come up here over Pinecone Hill," he traced a line with his paw, "and we'll work our way down to Prickle Thorn Corner. That's where I saw all those newfangled cans. With any luck, we'll be able to figure out how to open them, and be back home before the sun rises."

"Then," said Mother with satisfaction, "we can invite all the skunks and possums to a can-opening class. We'll teach them how to open those foolproof lids, we'll have a picnic supper, and we'll all be friends again!"

"Foolproof lids may really be foolproof," warned Grandfather.

"Pooh!" said Father. "No can is too hard for a smart raccoon to open."

There was a curious sound outside the kitchen, half way between a sneeze and a snicker. Albert and Arabella were sneaking past the door and they giggled when they heard Father. They knew who the smart raccoons were, and they

were on their way to Possum Junction
to prove it. Albert opened the front
door, and Arabella very carefully
lowered the latch so that it hardly made
a sound.

Inside the kitchen, Mother's sharp
ears pricked up. "Seems to be a lot of
stirring around tonight," she said ner-
vously.

"It's only the wind through the wil-
lows," said Father, and they settled
themselves to wait for the moon to go
down.

Albert and Arabella ran
down the path through
the woods. They tip-
toed past the rabbit hole
where Mrs. Rabbit's
babies were fast
asleep with their noses
on their paws.

They skirted the silvery pond where the
bullfrogs croaked hoarsely, "Here come
Rac—coons."

They glided as smoothly
as shadows through the
meadow while the
owl looking down
on them hooted,
"Here—Come—
Rac—coons!"

And they trotted hurriedly across the
road as the headlights of a car caught
the bright shine of their beady black
eyes.

When they got to Possum Junction, they did just as they had heard Father say. They sloshed through Duckweed Marsh with the tadpoles and peepers skip-hopping in front of them. They climbed stealthily up Pinecone Hill with the pine needles soft and slippery underfoot. And they worked their way down to Prickle Thorn Corner where all the newfangled cans with the fool-proof lids were.

When they got there it was very quiet. Some garbage cans were lined up in a row next to a garage, their foolproof lids locked on tight with handles that stuck up like ears.

The twins sniffed at all of the cans cautiously, and then singled out one that smelled especially good. Then Albert backed off, put his head down, and ran as fast as he could till his head butted THWOCK! against the can.

The can went over with a thud but the lid stayed on. Albert pulled and pried at the ear-shaped handles while Arabella got a toehold on the lid and pushed with all her might. It was no use. The lid stayed on. Then the twins ran round and round the can stopping every once in a while and standing on their tiptoes to examine the handles. After a while, they sat down to rest.

"If I had a long flat stick," said Albert thoughtfully, "I could put it through the handle and we would both sit on one end and work it like a seesaw. That way, when the stick went down, the handle would flip open."

Arabella jumped up and down excitedly. "That's what I call a smart raccoon!" she said. "Let's go look for a stick. You look out here, and I'll look inside the garage."

"OK," said Albert, and he ran off to look.

Arabella tiptoed into the garage. She saw a lawnmower, a ladder, an old trunk, and a bicycle. In front of her were some coils of rope, a box of old toys with blocks and dolls and roller skates spilling out, and a large empty pretzel can. In one corner were piles of newspapers, a sled, and some ice skates, and standing against the wall...a hockey stick!

chapter 3

Arabella squeaked in delight and ran forward eagerly to get the stick. In her haste she tripped on the coil of rope that was in front of her and somersaulted head over heels with a loud crash into the box of toys. Arabella lay very still for a moment. The crash had been loud enough for all the skunks and possums in Possum Junction to come and investigate. She pulled herself up cautiously and peered over the edge of the box. All was quiet.

Breathing a sigh of relief she stepped backwards out of the box, and immediately her foot was caught in something hard and cold that clamped on tight. Arabella looked down in horror and saw that she was attached to a roller skate. She shook her foot, but the skate stuck fast. She put her foot down hard and shoved.

Woosh! Away she went...arms outstretched, tail flying behind...Smack! into the empty pretzel can. The can flew up, looped in the air, and came down Spang! on her head. Wearing the can like a helmet, Arabella pirouetted gracefully and was flung like a top against the back wall. With a crash that shook the garage, she landed in a heap on the pile of newspapers. In the silence that followed, Arabella could hear far in the distance an angry murmuring.

Just then Albert ran into the garage. "Arabella!" he yelled, "There's a whole troop of skunks and possums coming down the hill...We've got to get the lid off the can fast!" He stopped short and stared at Arabella in amazement. She had pulled herself up and, balancing shakily on her skate, was brandishing the hockey stick like a sword in front of her.

"That's perfect, Arabella," Albert yelled in delight. "Just perfect!" Outside, the angry murmuring was coming closer.

"Quick," cried Arabella, "help me get the skate off."

"There's no time," said Albert. "They've got Mother and Father."

Much closer now, they heard Grandfather's voice, "We only want to show you..."

"WE'LL SHOW *YOU!*" yelled the skunks and the possums.

"They've got Grandfather too," gasped Arabella.

"You keep a good grip on the hockey stick," yelled Albert, "and aim it right at that garbage can. We'll show those skunks and possums!"

Albert ran in back of Arabella and
steered her down the length of the garage.
Arabella, zooming along on her roller
skate, aimed the hockey stick, business
end ready. Faster and faster they flew,
wooshing out of the garage into the very
midst of the roaring crowd. Arabella

struck wildly about her in all directions, clearing a path to the garbage can, sending the terrified skunks and possums flying.

"Get ready," yelled Albert. "Aim... NOW!"

With a sudden twist, Arabella hooked the hockey stick under the foolproof handle of the garbage can and sat down hard, putting all of her weight on the stick.

Albert jumped on top of her, adding his weight. The stick went down like a see-saw, and the foolproof handle flipped open! Immediately, the lid spun off and the twins were flung up into the air. They came down into the open garbage can with a thud that sent Arabella's roller skate flying and rattled the pretzel can loose from her head!

For a moment there was absolute silence. Inside the garbage can Arabella gingerly was feeling with her tongue an odd space that had suddenly appeared in her front teeth. She poked her head out of the can as Father, holding the lid of the foolproof garbage can aloft, said proudly to the startled skunks and possums, "I told you no can was too hard for a smart raccoon to open!" He reached over and patted Arabella on the head. "Albert," he said, "you twins did a fine job!"

"I'm not Albert, sir, I'm Arabella," said Arabella, and she grinned to show off the space where her front tooth had come out.

Albert poked his head out of the can. "I'm Albert, sir," he said.

Grandfather, standing at the edge of the crowd with Mother, looked hard at Albert. Then he stared at Arabella. "I told you," he said turning to Mother, "I told you all along! I told you that Nature was bound to take her course!"

That evening, the skunks and possums came to the twins' house for a can-opening class. Afterwards they all had a picnic supper. There were potato salad and baked beans, cole slaw and meat loaf, hot dogs and corn on the cob, relish and pickles, root beer, lemonade, and pitchers of cool foamy milk. For dessert there were the famous Possum Junction cream cakes and sticky buns. Arabella and Albert sat in the place of honor at the head of the picnic table.

Grandfather got up, cleared his throat and said, "Friends and neighbors, I have an announcement to make. Starting next week we will open a new sporting goods shop featuring foolproof garbage can openers. You'll be able to get a small, inexpensive model, or a special jumbo model with your name on it. Mother will be head sales lady, and I will be general manager. Father will be doing the whittling with the help of the twins. We guarantee that all the openers will work perfectly or your money back!"

A cheer went up from the crowd. Grandfather cleared his throat again. "If the twins can stop eating and drinking for a minute," he said looking at them fondly, "Now we can tell which is which...."

"You mean who is who," whispered Mother.

"Yes," said Grandfather, "now that we can tell Arabella from Albert, I'd like to

introduce the talented young designers of the New Foolproof Garbage Can Opener. Arabella your turn first."

Arabella lifted her nose out of her milk mug and stood up and curtsied and grinned.

Grandfather peered over his glasses at the space between her front teeth. "Now your turn, Albert."

Albert lifted his nose out of his milk mug. Then he took a last bite of sticky bun. An odd look came into his beady black eyes and he swallowed very hard. Then he stood up and bowed and grinned.

"Oh no!" said Grandfather sinking into his chair. "Oh no!"

For there, side by side, stood the twins looking exactly alike again.... The same number of rings on their tails, the same bright look in their beady black eyes, the same milk mustaches, and when they grinned, exactly the same space in their front teeth where a loose tooth had come out!